The Tender Trap

The
TENDER
TRAP

Oliver Cary

The Tender Trap

©2024 by Oliver Cary All rights reserved.

Published by Lulu Klewin

ISBN: 979-8-89021-252-8 Paperback
ISBN: 979-8-89021-253-5 Hardback
ISBN: 979-8-89021-251-1 eBook

Printed in the United States of America

This book is printed on acid-free paper.

CONTENTS

ACKNOWLEDGMENT

The world turns and the seasons change. It is the way of nature and the fundamental purpose of the Creator who designed and made this wonderful world in which we live and breed. Unfortunately, some elements are available to anyone who wishes to seek them out and to use them, which can and will disorient their minds, and turn their spirits from the original and purposeful way of being, to a way that is the opposite of what the Creator has designed them for.

I want to give thanks to my cousin, Ralph, who has given me the fortunate knowledge of the happenstance of the actual way this story unfolds. This story is a true happening of what happened in my own words.

Thank you to my significant other, Linda, who sat with me many nights editing and re-reading the pages as they came from my computer. I also want to give praise, glory, and honor to my creator who has given me the mental ability to put these thoughts together and present them to you, the general public.

I hope that you will enjoy and understand the story as it is and if it pleases you, I implore you to pass it on to someone that you think might be useful too.

Oliver

PREFACE

"To be or not to be, that is the question"

BY WILLIAM SHAKESPEARE
(*from* Hamlet, *spoken by Hamlet*)

"To be, or not to be, that is the question:
whether it is nobler in the mind to suffer
the slings and arrows of outrageous fortune,
or to take arms against a sea of troubles
and by opposing end them. To die-to sleep,
no more; and by a sleep to say we end
the heart-ache and the thousand natural shocks
the flesh is heir to."

Shakespeare wrote these few words. They had meaning and relevance to him at that time of writing them. They now have meaning andrelevance to me at this time of my writing. I look at the words in the poem and I transpose a few of them to say this;

"To do, or not to do,
to indulge, or not to indulge,
that is the question:
whether it is nobler in the mind to suffer
the slings and arrows of outrageous addiction,
which there are many,
or to take arms against the sea of troubles
and by opposing end them
to live and progress in a natural life.
To die, and to sleep,
no more; and by a sleep to say we end
the heart ache and the thousands of natural shocks that the flesh is heir
to because of
our indulgence with the drugs."

The choice was given to us, from birth. What we do with it is entirely up to us as individuals. Our lives are our own and during the space of time that we are alive, there is no interaction with anyone or anything that can undermine this, except the use of a mind and spirit altering drug. For anyone who is susceptible to the effects of these types of drugs, of which there are many, they will find that life is very difficult and arduous.

Their way will seem pleasurable at first but will then progress into something out of control.

Big oak trees grow from little acorns. When the little seed is planted it spreads its roots underground and then it pierces the surface and begins to grow. As it grows it takes on the shape and form of the large tree. The large tree gathers the strength it needs to continue on its journey through life. This is very symbolic of the way drugs evolve. They gain strength through their use, by people, and on and on it goes. Knowledge of the drugs and how they perpetuate Is the way of overcoming them.

This story is a step in the right direction to gain knowledge and also to learn how to overcome the effects and utilization of them. There is an old saying by a person that was one of the stars in the show Star Trek, his name was Spock. The saying was **"Live long and Prosper."**

CHAPTER 1

As life goes on, it becomes increasingly obvious that one is a lonely number and it seems as though my life is heading that way. My wife of fifteen years, had recently passed away due to heart failure. For several months she had been going in for treatments to help her sustain the effects of the disease, but finally it overcame her. I started taking long walks in the evening to keep my weight in order and to pass the time.

It is late in the evening on the coldest day of the year and I find myself walking along the north main street in Providence RI. As I covered the distance from the bus station and downtown, which was about a mile, I began to feel an irritating hunger in my stomach. I stopped at one of the local eateries which was called, New York System. I bought two hot wieners and a soda and sat down in a booth to devour my "scrumptious" meal.

As I sat in my booth, eating the meal, I began to reminisce about the days gone by, before I married my wife, when I had the choice of fine, beautiful ladies who loved to keep me company and enjoy a meal or two and even want to have sex with me. Well, that was then, and this is now. I remembered the many times that my fortune had been turned around and I had been given the chance to start all over again. Fortunately, the good Lord blessed me with a discerning mind and a vivid imagination.

You see, this is a story about how I fell from God's grace and from the top of my industry, which was automobile sales and refurbishing. For 11 years, I enjoyed the opportunity to sell high end vehicles to the cream of society. I also furnished my clientele with expert workmanship on the vehicles when they needed my services. I inherited a wonderful business sense from my late and great father. He owned the business before me. When he passed on, I inherited it. He was a great mechanic and he loved to work on cars that he bought from auction sales or on his own. I learned how to maintain vehicles from his ability. I even started drag racing cars, at a race track in Colchester CT. This led me to meet and greet those people who were connected, and my business began to grow. I was able to start supplying high end vehicles and I offered quality automobile services. All of which, placed me and my company into an echelon of society that enabled me to live a very comfortable life style.

Due to the type of people that I was in contact with, I became invited to many social events and I got to meet and know people of influence who had their hands in a lot of situations, some of which became interesting to me, sometimes, too interesting!!!!!

My personality was very amiable and I was liked by almost everyone that I met. My clients were very sociable and held a lot of parties which I was invited to attend. Parties began to be a part of my lifestyle and traveling to the different places that my new found friends went to, also became an ongoing thing.

Of course, as I stated before, this story is about my fall from grace and the from top of my industry. The partying began to take a toll on my business. I was able to maintain it for a while, but there was another factor which came into play, and it was the one thing that began to destroy what I had built. Don't get me wrong, I am not a fool nor am I stupid. But, when you mix cocaine and sex together, it is truly unbearable to overcome. The pleasure of achieving the ultimate orgasm under the influence of a pleasure enhancing drug, is something many people search for. At least those who have been or are involved with that side of life, search for. Of course, that, along with having the company of a beautiful "sex goddess" by your side to enjoy it all with, is an experience I will bring to bear as I proceed to tell my story.

I didn't know at the time that I would need to overcome the attraction to both of those things, sex, and cocaine. But, as time went on, I learned the hard way. That is correct, you read the words correctly, sex and cocaine.

Let me inform you of which came first, sex, sex, sex!

CHAPTER 2

You see, I was present at a really nice party, having a good time. I was standing at the bar ordering a drink. As I turned my head to the left, I saw a vision of the utmost beauty walking past me. She was the most beautiful woman I had ever seen. She was about 5'8" tall, with a slender waist, a well-rounded butt, well-shaped legs, large breasts, and blonde hair, which was very beautifully styled. It was a reflex action for me to try to start a conversation with her. I said to her, "excuse me, miss, but i must say that I have never seen, or met a woman as beautiful as you! May I introduce myself?" She answered, "yes." "I said my name is, Andre, what is your name?," and she responded with "hello, Andre. My name is Layla. It's nice to meet you."

The night went on and we continued to communicate and I told her what I did for a living and she responded with what she did, which was, dancing. That explained her fabulous physique, because only a person who goes to the gym 2 or 3 times a week, or one who dances for a living, could maintain such a high caliber of fitness. I became totally enthralled with her grace and poise. So, it was getting late and we both decided that we would call it a night. We exchanged phone numbers and I walked her to her vehicle, a Mercedes Benz, and she left. I felt surprisingly good that night after meeting her. I went to my hotel room and poured myself a night cap and went to bed with a smile on my face, hoping that we would meet again.

Not wanting to seem overzealous, I waited for two days to call her. I dialed her number and she answered immediately. I said "Hi, Layla, this is Andre." She responded with "Hi Andre, I was just thinking about you.

How are you doing?" I said "I am doing very well; I have been thinking about you and the conversation that we had the other night. Would you like to meet again? I would love to take you to dinner." She responded, "Sure, that would be nice." I said, "are you free this evening?" She responded "Yes, I am free." I said "I will pick you up at 7:00. What is your address?" She said "1441 Garden Drive. It is located in the Garden City condominiums. I am in apartment number 1208. See you then, she said in an overly sweet and amicable tone."

As the day went on, I was on cloud nine. I no longer had the "oh me blues" and my future was looking up. Thank God!!!

CHAPTER 3

At my business, the men were hard at work and the cars were being pumped out in fun time. Two transmission services were being done, there were three fender repairs and also there were three paint jobs that were being done. It was Wednesday, commonly known as "hump day," and I was in the office going over the books and writing out paychecks to pass out to the workers later that day.

I decided to call the florist, who was just a few blocks away, and I ordered a small bouquet. I also called and made reservations at Hemenway's Restaurant. After I closed the shop down, I went to pick up the flowers and then went home to shave and bathe and put on something nice. After getting myself together, it was time to call Layla.

6:55 pm

"Hi, I hope you don't mind that I am a few minutes early. I am a stickler for being on time, if not a few minutes early for my appointments."

"Hi, oh no, I am quite happy that you are a little early. That lets me know that you honor your commitments and you care about other people's time."

"Are you ready?"

"Yes, I am ready. I will meet you downstairs in my lobby, okay" "Great, I will be there in 10 minutes."

7:05

I was at her condominium just as I promised and she walked out of the elevator looking like a Greek goddess, dressed in black slacks, with a turquoise blouse that came to her waist just above her belly button, and a waist-length silver leather jacket. She was gorgeous!!!!!

I stepped out of my car opened the passenger door for her and handed her the flowers, she thanked me and said the flowers were beautiful as she entered into my car. As she stepped past me, I couldn't help but notice the fragrance that she wore. I asked her what brand of perfume she was wearing and she said, "Mademoiselle by Chanel, do you like it?" I replied, "Yes, I do, most definitely. That happens to be my favorite fragrance." I got in the car, closed the door, and we went away.

7:30 pm

Having made reservations at Hemenways Restaurant, I drove up to the valet car park and was received very quickly and cordially. Hemenways is an upscale establishment that is renowned for serving great food with excellent service.

Upon arriving at the door, the valet came over and greeted me by my name and said that he was glad to see me again. I tipped him and we went inside. As we entered inside, the maitre'd walked up and shook my hand and he also called me by my name and said how pleasant it was to have us at the restaurant, then he escorted us to my usual table. You see, as a successful business owner in the area, I was accustomed to dining at the restaurant quite often with my clients and friends so, it was not unusual that the staff would recognize me and acknowledge me personally.

The waiter came over and asked if we would care for a cocktail. We ordered martinis and talked as we looked at the menu. As I mentioned before, the choice of food is terrific so we took our time going over the menu. I ordered six oysters in the half shell and Layla ordered a shrimp cocktail for our appetizers. For our entrees, Layla ordered Lobster Mac and Cheese, and I ordered Paella. We ate and enjoyed our meal as we talked and began to get to know each other. We ordered another round of drinks, and without having any dessert, because we were quite full, we decided to leave. I paid the bill and waited for my vehicle to come up. I tipped the driver again and drove off.

This meal was quite more satisfying than the one I had at the New York System the other day, after all, the good Lord blessed me with the company of the most beautiful woman I ever laid my eyes on, sitting across from me at the dinner table.

It was still early and we both were feeling good, so I asked her if she would like to go to a jazz club to hear some music. She said, "Absolutely, I love jazz." Earlier on, she had been married to a jazz musician and grew to love music. I told her, "I had been married and my wife and I were avid fans of jazz. We often went to clubs and listened to the groups that played." She asked me "Are you still married" and I said, "No, she passed away two years ago." She asked, "From what" "She had a bad heart and kidney failure." Then I said, "Enough of that, let's go hear some good music" and off we went. As the time being early, I put my Cadillac on 95 northbound and headed to Boston Mass.

We arrived at the club, which was called Sculler's Jazz Club, just in time for the first set. It just so happened that one of my favorite performers, Marc Cary, was going on stage with his band. I had the opportunity to hear Marc and his group perform in New York City. He recognized me in the audience. When he saw me, he acknowledged me and Layla. That was genuinely nice of him. Then he dedicated the first tune that the group played, which was "Mr. Lucky," to me and Layla. It seemed as though the night was perfect the way things fell into place. We stayed to listen to another set and then we bid Marc, and the members of the band, farewell and left. I drove back to Providence and on the way, we held hands and talked about how nice the evening was.

I reached Layla's condominium and we shared an endearing kiss. I opened the door for her, and we both agreed that we should do that again. Layla went inside and I got into my car and drove off. The night was one that I won't easily forget. In fact, I will never forget the way she looked when she sauntered out of the elevator, or that wonderful fragrance which she wore, Mademoiselle by Chanel. Wow.....

CHAPTER 4

I spent the next few days engrossed in my business. I had acquired a few new patrons who purchased a new Audi and a new Maserati. It was my job to give the vehicles a clean bill of health from top to bottom. I had the men, who work for me, put the cars to the test for diagnostics and driving performance. Everything went well and I was able to deliver the vehicles with my seal of approval. Not a moment went by that I didn't think about, beautiful, Layla. It had been two days since we had seen each other or even spoken over the phone. It was then that I was startled by my cell phone. I looked at the caller ID and saw that it was Layla. I answered and said, "Hi, how are you?" She responded, "Hi, I am doing well." I continued by saying, "It is nice to hear your voice. Of course, this may sound a little cliche, but I have been thinking about you. I am glad that you called."

I had been fantasizing about her whenever I had a free moment and I wasn't preoccupied with work or something else. She said, "The evening that we spent together seemed like it might have been too good to be true, and I would like to see you again to be able to understand whether or not you are a real person or just a figment of my imagination." We both chuckled at what she said, and I responded, "Of course we can, is there something you had in mind that you would like to do?"

She stated, "I have a friend who is having a get-together on his yacht which he keeps moored in Watch Hill Rhode Island. It is going to be a small gathering to celebrate his company's signing of a big contract with Taylor Swift, the pop star entertainer, who has recently purchased property in the Watch Hill area. Would you like to go?" I said, "Yes, I would love to attend the party with you. This will allow me to meet some of your friends. That will be fun!! When is the party going to be?" She said, "It will be this weekend, Saturday and Sunday." "Okay, what is the dress code for this occasion?" "Slacks, sports jacket, and whatever you wear to go with that, will be fine." "No problem, what time does it start?" She said, "It will begin around 7:00 with a cruise around the bay and then something to eat." I said "I will come and get you around 6:00, see you then. Ciao bella."

CHAPTER 5

Saturday rolled around and I arrived at Layla's to pick her up around 6:00. She was putting on finishing touches and then she met me in the lobby just as before. We settled into the vehicle and drove off. It was a distance to Watch Hill, but the ride was pleasant and the weather was magnificent.

When we arrived at the yacht, a few of the other guests were already there. We walked up the gangplank and as soon as Jonathan, the person hosting the party, saw Layla, he came over and gave her a big hug and a kiss on the cheek. She then introduced me and we shook hands. Then he said, "Welcome, come on board and grab yourselves something to drink and enjoy the festivities."

Everyone seemed to be very friendly. Layla introduced me to the group and the evening began. Great sounds were being played by a local band that Jonathan hired and a chef who was cooking on a Hibachi grill out on the deck. The night was wonderful and of course, it was all being enhanced by the flowing beauty of the person that I had on my arm, Layla.

As the night went on, we danced, ate, and drank fine champagne. There was a very pleasant ambiance developing between Layla and myself as we held each other in our arms. I was becoming even more captivated by her fragrance and now that I held her in my arms, the feeling of an intense desire began to build. I could tell that she had the same feelings as me. The night rolled on and we were having a wonderful time. We began to think about leaving, so we found our way to the host of the party and thanked him for his hospitality and we left.

While we drove into the night air with the stars shining through the moon roof, the feelings that had been manifesting were still very much present prompting us to go the next step. As I drove up to Layla's condo, she said, "Would you like to come up for a nightcap?" Of course, I said "yes" and that is when we took off on the next part of our relationship.

CHAPTER 6

Layla's condominium was laid out with lavish furniture carpeting and other items that defined her character and personality. As we entered the living room door, she turned and caressed me by holding my hand and kissed me gently on my cheek, and then she told me that "the evening was wonderful and I had a very nice time." She asked, "What would you care to drink?" I said, "Gin and tonic would be fine." There was a mini bar set up in the far corner with a few chairs. I went over and sat down while she prepared the drinks.

After she placed the drink in front of me she excused herself and said she was going to freshen up and to make myself at home. I went over to the couch and the audio system that was set up on the other side of the room and tuned in a smooth jazz station, then I sat down and relaxed. A little while passed and shortly after Layla came back into the room. She had showered and changed into a black and red negligee that looked as though it was made for no one but her. It showed every curve on her body and it made her look even more glamorous than before. She came over to me and I reached my hand out and touched her breast, fondled her waist, and pulled her close. As I held her in my arms, we kissed and caressed each other. Then I said, "I would like to freshen up, after dancing and partying through the night." She showed me where the shower was and I undressed and stepped into it.

After I was through, I toweled off and walked into the next room which was her bedroom. Layla was lying on the bed with a glass tray next to her, which had some white powder on it. She asked if I would like some coke.

I had never tried any coke before and I didn't see any harm, I said, "Sure, why not."

The coke served to heighten the sexual sensations as Layla and I enjoyed each other's embraces. It just so happened that we enjoyed each other so much that we began to become inseparable. Repeatedly we climaxed in earth-shattering orgasms. We had quite a physical and sexual relationship, and it was everything that I dreamed would be better. I did not know the tremendous effect the coke(cocaine) had on me until years later.

We did things together; went places together; made friends together; and shared things until the time came when she told me that she had to move out of her condominium. Little did I know that her condo fees were being paid for by her "sugar daddy."

The person who was the "sugar daddy" no longer wanted to be involved with her and stopped paying for everything. This left Layla on her own with nowhere to turn. I saw that she needed help, so because of our relationship, I told her that she could move in with me. You see I had a large house that I acquired when my wife was alive. It was a four-bedroom Mediterranean-style house with a tennis court, a three-car garage, and a swimming pool. There was an expansive garden that my dearly deceased wife loved to propagate.

Of course, Layla put up a slight opposition, but that did not last exceptionally long. She declined several times. I knew that she had nowhere to turn so I gently coerced her, at least that is what I thought I was doing, into staying with me. I knew that way I could be assured of having her close to me anytime I wanted and our sex life would not suffer. After a little while, she submitted and said okay that she would move in with me. Little did I realize that cocaine was also moving along with her, into my life. I had already become addicted to having sex with the most beautiful and sexually attractive woman I had ever known, as well as, using the most habitual and intoxicating drug known to man.

One thing led to another and pretty soon, as time moved on, Layla and I began to drift apart. She began going on short vacations to my house in Florida and staying for weeks at a time. She spent more time with her "girl-friends," and our sex life was not as vibrant as before. My business began to take a downfall and I started losing clients and some of my workers quit and went to other dealerships. So, realizing that time was not on my side, I took some time off and checked myself into a rehabilitation facility in Arizona. Before leaving and going to the rehabilitation facility, I hired a construction person to work on some parts of my house and fix some items that had fallen into disarray. His name was Octavio. He was of Spanish descent and he came with particularly good references.

The cocaine was taking its toll on me, although it didn't seem to affect Layla at all. To top it off, I started to lose my ability to perform as sexually as before. She was still as sexy and flexible as before. Of course, I had the receipts for all of the spa work that she attended and body work that she had done, to keep her that way. I didn't realize it then, but I do now. Before I went away, I also took this time to hire a private detective to follow her document her activities, and record who she was seeing. I also gave the detective a key to my house and a blank check so that he could purchase top-notch electronic surveillance equipment. I instructed him to place the cameras and equipment strategically all around my house. He did that while Layla was going out to her appointments and spa services.

I stayed at the facility for a month, adhering to all the stipulations that were given to me. During this time, Layla stayed at the house. The construction worker was doing his work and the private detective was able to work around all that was going on with Layla coming in and out as well as the construction workers. My plan worked out without a hitch. When I returned home from the rehabilitation facility, I overheard Layla talking on the telephone to one of her friends. They were talking about a man to whom they were both attracted. This gave me some clarity about why my sex life was not as active as it was when I first met Layla. So, I had to decide what I was going to do about it. During the time that Layla and I were together, I had purchased property in Florida. On the property, there was a house with a two-car garage, a swimming pool, a tennis court, and all the amenities. Occasionally Layla would travel down there and spend some time there. I didn't think anything of it, but now that I had overheard her conversation, It made me wonder.

The private investigator followed her to find out just what was going on. He kept records of people she met, where she shopped, and more. I had every part of Layla's life documented as well as photographed. You see, I had my house arranged with cameras all over, to record the actions going on in my house. I realized that you can never be too cautious with yourself when you are dealing with a drug-abusing woman or man. No matter how beautiful they may appear to be, that is only the cover not the inside of the person. I am sure you have heard the saying; "Never judge a book by its cover," Well, having fallen victim to the curse of judging a book by its cover, I began to take action to protect myself.

One day, I invited some friends over to the house for dinner and a movie night. You see there was a movie theatre next to the dining area. I invited my friend Ralph, who was a trusted and close friend, Theodore, the bouncer at the nearby strip club, who was also a trusted and close friend, my lawyer Maxim, Reggie my chauffeur, and Theodore who was my bodyguard. Of course, the lady of the house, Layla, her mother and, oh yes, I can't forget Octavio, the person who did all of the renovation and modernization of my homestead.

All of this was for a reason soon to be revealed. After dinner, as everyone entered the viewing area, they were handed a dossier containing documents and were asked to sit in pre-assigned seats. After everyone was comfortable the movie clicked on. When the scene started, a naked woman's figure appeared on the screen, with her buttocks facing the camera. It happened pretty quickly, but my friend, Ralph, caught the fact of what he saw and knew who it was, and he said with quickness, "Hey, hey, I think you have the wrong film going on." I responded with a quickness, "No, Ralph. I have exactly the correct film. The film you are looking at is one of my beautiful naked woman who is walking through my house and is naked in front of her naked lover." Shortly after the first scene came the next one of a naked man slowly walking toward Layla. He stopped when he reached her and held her close to himself and started sucking on her nipples. He just happened to be the construction man, Octavio. "This was the lover that I had mentioned earlier."

Wow!!!!, what a night this was turning out to be. At that moment, all eyes turned toward Layla and Octavio. Layla jumped out of her chair and started screaming "Turn it off, turn it off !!!" But Andre was adamant about showing up his woman for the person she really was and the show went on. The footage ran for another 15 minutes while everyone sat there with their mouths open and their eyes glued to the screen.

Layla started crying and apologizing to Andre. Saying "I don't know what got into me, honey. It was only those few times that Octavio and I were together. Please forgive me. It will never ever happen again. You know that I love you."

Andre retorted " Bitch, Shut your filthy lying ass mouth. I have cameras in every corner of this house." Andre even had footage of the two doing cunnilingus and fellatio with each other. The cameras photographed them in almost every room in the house, especially in his Master Bedroom where Layla and he made love and slept. This infuriated Andre, that she had entertained another man in his house and his bed. He said, "I had this house laid out with the best cameras and microphones money could buy. I have you and your lover photographed for the past 30 days, running around this house sucking and fucking in practically every room. Not only do I have the photos of you and him, but there are explicit audio recordings in which you told your girlfriends about how much you hated being touched by me and that you wished I would die. I also have it on tape that you and your friends thought Octavio was such a fantastic lover. I have recordings of all of you sniffing and using cocaine, in quantity. I also want you to know that you hold in your hands documentation of everything you have seen on the screen as well as the recorded conversations with you and your girlfriends in restaurants and places you meet. I have a recording in which you and your girlfriends were collaborating to kill me. You made the statement that you couldn't wait for me to die." Layla then asked, "How do you know that?" Andre said, "Because the private detective that I hired was sitting in a booth directly behind you at the Cowesett Inn when you were talking to your friends and said that to them."

At this point, Layla's mother chimed in, and with disgust on her face, said "What have you done, stupid girl? This man has been so wonderful to both of us. Now you have used and embarrassed him." Layla's mother became irate and started cursing at her daughter, for you see, Andre not only housed and kept Layla, but he also paid for her mother's Audi A3.

They were both living high on the hog, so to speak, at Andre's expense. Now, that was very soon, going to end. As all of this was transpiring, Octavio sat silently. At this point, he wanted to get up and leave. But Andre overruled his leaving and directed him to sit back down and said I'm not finished yet!!!!."

Octavio said to Andre, "You owe me $13,000." Andre replied, "You say that I owe you $13,000? Okay just a moment, I will get my checkbook." Andre went and obtained his checkbook and wrote out a check for the $13,000 and handed the check to Theodore, the bouncer. Now, Theodore has your check. If he gives it to you, okay." Octavio looked at Theodore and saw the menacing look on his face as well as his muscle bond physique and decided not to go after the check. Instead, Octavio quickly got up from his seat and left out of the house to get into his truck to leave. At that time Ralph followed him outside and grabbed him by the collar and said, "Listen and listen well. That man is my friend! If you ever come back here for anything, and I hear about it, you are going to have a problem with me. Do you understand me!" Octavio "timidly said yes, I understand" and he left.

When Ralph went back into the house everyone was standing around and talking. Layla's mother brought up the subject of what happens to her daughter now. Unbeknownst to Andre, Layla's mother had secretly dialed the police. Andre heard the doorbell. He asked his daughter, who had come to stay with him, to answer the door. Upon opening the door, she announced that the police were at the door. When the police entered the room, Andre asked them "What is the problem" The police said, "We received a call from this location that there was a problem here." Then the police saw Ralph and asked him "Hey you, what are you doing here?" You see, Ralph was the only Black person in the room and Andre's house was in a well-known white residential area of the city. Andre immediately spoke up and said, "This man is my friend and I want him here. This is my house. In fact, let me introduce you to my attorney. This is Maxim Fienstien." Maxim then presented his business card to the police and spoke to them. Soon afterward, the police told Andre, "Please pardon the intrusion. If you have any more problems don't hesitate to call us, goodnight." and they left.

Now Andre continued, directing his attention to Layla, "As for you, I want you out of this house tonight!" Layla's mother said, "But she has nowhere to go" Andre said, "I have taken care of that. I have planned for you to stay in a hotel room for a month. The hotel room is paid for.

That should give you enough time to find yourself another place to live or whatever you intend to do. I want you to get your things and leave this house tonight. I have been sleeping with a pistol under my pillow for 6 months since I heard you and your friends talking about killing me.

I do not want you near me or in this house one more night. I am thinking about giving you some money to keep your head above water. I haven't decided how much money I am willing to give you but I will decide on that and let you know. Now, you have one of two choices; 1) if you leave tonight, I will give you the money and you have a place to stay for a month that is paid for. 2) If you stay in this house tonight, I won't give you a dime, and everything you have here you will lose. What are you going to do?"

CHAPTER 7

A wise choice was made. Layla and her mother went upstairs and packed up what they could carry her clothes and jewels, and then they came back downstairs and then out to her mother's vehicle. Thinking about the way things went down that night, I tend to feel honored to know a person like Andre. You see, he displayed a strong character in as much as he held back the anger and rage that he must have felt toward the woman he had fallen in lust with. Using the substance that controlled and enhanced his sexual inclinations was his way of enjoying her and in some way controlling her. Andre did promise that he would supply Layla with some money. Being the honorable man that he was, he gave her a check for $5,000.00. He had already paid for a place for her to stay for a month and he never saw or heard from her again.

CHAPTER 8

By using the drug cocaine, it always gives one the feeling of overwhelming superiority and enhances the sexual abilities of the user, most of the time. But the unnatural and synthetic means of achieving the ultimate feeling that gives the type of pleasure to a person that they are searching for, will always fade and disappear.

Why do you think the natural order of things is to grow, flower, fade, and die? Then begin the cycle again with another seed or stem; or another baby or adult that carries the essence of what the flower represents. That is what Andre fell in lust with, not the flower itself. It is impossible to possess or even capture the flower or the essence itself because it will always perpetuate itself. Repeatedly, the flower blooms and the desire appears. The essence may appear in many forms, shapes, and sizes. When it does appear, one usually embraces it because it gives the presence of what one desires. A person must remember that evil can take on whatever face or mannerism that a person desires. Believe that the essence is exceptionally smooth, stealthy, and crafty. Remember how Layla induced Andre to have a portion of the forbidden essence which was, "Would you like some coke?" Initially, Andre was captivated by the overwhelming presence of beauty, Layla, after which the use of coke enhanced his feelings. The beauty that he held in his subconscious had been realized, in his mind's eye, and he was unable to detach himself from it. The essence of it grew and attached itself to him, and he enjoyed it, as long as his health and mental capacity would allow.

Fortunately, the good and merciful Lord and Creator of our universe has implanted in our make-up, also known as DNA, a stop-gap, that when triggered, will cause us to stop the process of self-degradation. Of course, this doesn't work on everyone because of what is known as, "FREE WILL." When free will is in play the person is at a disadvantage. This is because they are human. Humanity itself has a single fault, which will continue until the end of time, and that fault is "self-indulgence." Once any human understands that the importance of the indulgence of the fault is the downfall of themselves as a rational and sensible person, then and only then will we begin to grab and hold onto the essence of life itself.

The essence is LOVE. We need to understand what the essence of Love is and where it stems from. In my understanding of the life that I have lived and of the life that I now live, I believe and I know it comes from my relationship with JESUS, the one and only son of God. He is the only person that has been born, who died, and was brought back to life again by the very will of GOD himself. JESUS is the essence of LOVE. His teachings and exhortations are all about LOVE. There is no animosity in his teachings nor is there any hatred or any ill intent. If I had continued the path of using drugs and partaking in the sexual activities that were inherent in my life, I would have died. For you see, I virtually lived the life that Andre did. Andre, very much like myself, found the path that led him back to sanity. This enabled him to overcome his dependence on that drug, which he could not do while under the influence of the drug. If you look at the way Andre ended the relationship with Layla, he used the helping aid of other people who were insensitive to the inundations of the drug, itself, and sex. He took himself out of harm's way and left the environment of people, places, and things. He learned that no one could do what needed to be done but himself and with the Holy Spirit leading him into all truth, he was able to do that.

Once he returned he was able to combat the demon and defeat the minions that were overwhelming his presence of mind and destroying his relationship with his creator. Once he removed the tool that was infringing upon his mental and spiritual faculties and was able to focus, then and only then did he understand the essence of his life was not found in drugs or sex, but in the glorious environment with GOD, Himself. The exquisite presence of the creator will not allow anything or anyone that is not pure heart and honesty. Andre had to become honest with himself before he could be the one to bring honesty into his relationship with Layla.

Otherwise, Layla would have been able to keep hold of the reigns of power over him through subterfuge (action taken, or maneuvers made, to evade, conceal, or obscure).

CHAPTER 9

Upon becoming honest and eliminating the use of the cocaine along with the resistance to the desire of having sex with Layla, another factor has entered Andre's life. That is the presence of loneliness. The previous objects that were eliminated, i.e.. Layla, drugs, and sex have left a void in Andre's life. Little did he know that he would have the time that it took to use those things, at his disposal. What does he do with that time? The void must be filled with good and wholesome objectives in order to stop the recurrence of his old habits.

One day William, a friend of Andre, invited him to go to a meeting. His friend was involved in the organization of NA, Narcotics Anonymous. Andre had previously been introduced to the NA organization while in the rehabilitation facility in Arizona. Andre agreed to attend the meeting with him.

It was a cold snowy night, November 12, when Andre and William drove into the parking lot of the NA meeting hall. It didn't look extravagant but it was the place that became "the beginning of the rest of Andre's life." When they walked into the room, Andre immediately felt a feeling of peace sweep over him. People were sharing their stories about their use of drugs and how they overcame or were struggling to overcome, the use of them. Some of the situations that were shared seemed close, but not exactly like his. At that time, he came to realize that everyone's experience was singular to themselves, just like his experience was singular to him. He enjoyed meeting with people who shared remarkably similar circumstances to what he did. It made him feel like part of a family, the Narcotics Anonymous family.

¶Andre started attending regular meetings. He completed the stipulated 90 meetings in 90 days. He received his NA coins which denoted that he was clean and sober for a certain length of time and he did not use any drug or alcohol. His character was changing and he involved himself in affairs that did not allow him to be associated with people that were using them or go to places where people may be using them. His lifestyle had changed and he was happy that it did.

With these changes, his business began an upswing. New customers are coming and life is looking better. He opened two other dealerships. His workers were more attentive and their quality of work improved. This was all due to the Grace of God, and Andre's strength and ability to stop the use of drugs. A brief time passed, and Andre met a young lady. Her name was Suzette. She was also in the NA program.

They met often and had lunch and sometimes dinner with each other. They liked each other and soon became attached as a couple and fell in love. Because they were in the NA program, this of course meant that there were no drugs or alcohol involved in their relationship. I bring this point up because what would be the use of NA if there were drugs or alcohol involved? None!

To bring this to a close, Andre and Suzette got married. Andre's business is going great and he travels quite a bit to vacation in different parts of the world with his wife. All and all, life is now worth living for Andre and he has brought joy and happiness into the lives of others. His happiness and sanctity of mind and spirit have been achieved by not using drugs and not allowing sex to control his passionate nature. You can do the same.

Psalms 34:19

"Many are the afflictions of the righteous: but the Lord delivereth him out of them all."

**If Jonah came out
of the great fish,
Daniel came out
of the lion's den,
and Lazarus came
out of the tomb,
you will also come
out of your problems.
If you believe, Amen**

Printed in the USA
CPSIA information can be obtained
at www.ICGtesting.com
CBHW070712121024
15570CB00001BA/17